Farmer
Dray's
farm

Apple Tree
Station

Apple Tree
Village

Church

School

Farmyard Tales

The Silly Sheepdog

Heather Amery

Adapted by Rob Lloyd Jones

Illustrated by Stephen Cartwright

Reading consultant: Alison Kelly

Find the duck on every double page.

This story is about
Apple Tree Farm,

Sam,

Poppy,

Ted,

a boy,

Woolly,

and Patch.

One morning, Mrs. Boot, Sam and Poppy were collecting firewood.

Ted came in his truck. "I've got a new sheepdog," he said.

His name is Patch.

"Can you show Patch
the sheep?" Ted asked.

"Those aren't
sheep, Patch."

"Those aren't
sheep either!"

"Oh Patch!
Those are *pigs*."

"Stop being such
a silly sheepdog!"
said Sam.

"*These* are the sheep,"
said Poppy.

"But Woolly
is missing!"

Patch barked...
and ran off.

He ran to a boy who
had found Woolly.

"Patch used to live on my parents' farm," the boy said.

"He's not a very
good sheepdog is
he?" said Sam.

The boy whistled...

...and Patch chased
Woolly into the field.

"Patch is a great
sheepdog," said
the boy.

You just have
to whistle.

"Thanks for your help,"
said Ted.

"Patch isn't a silly sheepdog after all," said Sam.

Puzzles

Puzzle 1

Choose the best speech bubble for each picture:

A.

Puzzle 2

Put the six pictures in order.

A

B

C

D

E

F

Puzzle 3

Can you spot six differences
between these two pictures?

Puzzle 4

How many chickens can you count in this picture?

How many sheep?

Puzzle 5

Fill in the missing word.

Woolly whistled pigs sheep

A.

"Those aren't
_____ either!"

B.

"Those are
_____."

C.

"But _____
is missing!"

D.

The boy
_____.

Answers to puzzles

Puzzle 1

A.

B.

C.

Puzzle 2

1A 2D 3E

4B 5F 6C

Puzzle 3

Puzzle 4
A. There are
   5 chickens.

B. There are
   7 sheep.

Puzzle 5
A. "Those aren't <u>sheep</u> either!"
B. "Those are <u>pigs</u>."
C. "But <u>Woolly</u> is missing!"
D. The boy <u>whistled</u>.

Designed by Laura Nelson
Series editor: Lesley Sims
Series designer: Russell Punter
Digital manipulation by
Nick Wakeford and John Russell

This edition first published in 2016 by Usborne Publishing Ltd.,
Usborne House, 83-85 Saffron Hill, London EC1N 8RT, England.
www.usborne.com Copyright © 2016, 1992 Usborne Publishing Ltd.

USBORNE FIRST READING
Level Two

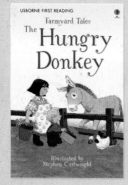

USBORNE FIRST READING
Farmyard Tales
The **Hungry Donkey**
Illustrated by Stephen Cartwright

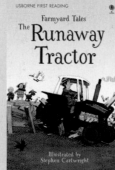

USBORNE FIRST READING
Farmyard Tales
The **Runaway Tractor**
Illustrated by Stephen Cartwright

USBORNE FIRST READING
Farmyard Tales
The **Naughty Sheep**
Illustrated by Stephen Cartwright

USBORNE FIRST READING
Farmyard Tales
Tractor in Trouble
Illustrated by Stephen Cartwright

Farmyard Tales
Kitten's Day Out
Illustrated by Stephen Cartwright

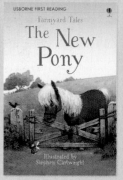

USBORNE FIRST READING
Farmyard Tales
The **New Pony**
Illustrated by Stephen Cartwright

USBORNE FIRST READING
Farmyard Tales
Pig Gets Lost
Illustrated by Stephen Cartwright

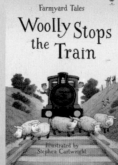

USBORNE FIRST READING
Farmyard Tales
Woolly Stops the Train
Illustrated by Stephen Cartwright

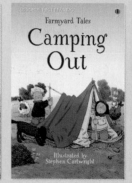

USBORNE FIRST READING
Farmyard Tales
Camping Out
Illustrated by Stephen Cartwright